Olivia Magnus is an 11 year old school girl with a great flair for writing. She is a massive bookworm and outstretches herself to discover new things. She would always read every night before bed and would imagine she was part of the story. Her mum always had faith in her to write a book and during lockdown, Olivia thought it to be the perfect time to become an author! As well as her love to books, she loves to perform on stage and see musicals whenever she can. She also enjoys gaming and coding, and hopes she makes her own video game someday.

THE DIFFERENCE IS THAT I AM DIFFERENT

Olivia Magnus

Illustrations by Andrés Rojas

CHAPTER 1
THE MEET UP

The stars in the sky barely glowed as Violet Johnson walked down the streets. She thought she was all alone until she saw something that attracted her tired eyes. It looked like a figure in the darkness. 'Who could be watching her?' she thought to herself. Violet blinked hard. However, as soon as her eyes opened, the figure she had previously seen wasn't there anymore! She began to get a little creeped out and was about to call her mum when she saw a head poking out of the alleyway. It looked like a kid, about her age, and was wearing a red cloak. She decided it was best to go and ask if they were OK, so she ran down the streets and turned to face a small trash can.

A young boy was kneeling down, hiding himself from Violet.

His blonde, spiky hair was poking out of his dark blue beanie. His pitch-black trainers were covered in mud and garbage. His red cloak had odd, grey lines on the back as if to reveal a hidden message. He turned to face Violet and stared into her dark, hazel eyes. He was no ordinary boy and Violet could tell. There was something strange about him, which seemed to poke out from under his cloak. He was wearing something quite odd, which was supposed to be put underneath the trousers. Something called....Underpants!

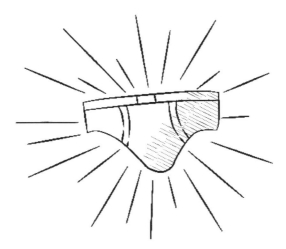

"Who are you?" Violet asked, shaking in fear.

"Who are you, if I may ask?" said the boy, pulling down his cloak and worried Violet could see.

"I asked first!" she said.

"OK fine! My name is Peter Simons, yours?"

"Violet. Violet Johnson."

Peter sniggered.

"You have a strange laugh, like some sort of..." she gasped.

"Are you a...wizard?"

"No, definitely not! Why would you say that?"

"In Harry Hotter, it says wizards wear cloaks and have very stupid laughs. So, I just guessed."

"Are you mocking me?"

"Of course, not!" she lied.

"Girls are so stupid," mumbled Peter. Violet gave him a stare.

"What? I was just saying!"

"Anyway," said Violet, trying to change the subject. "It's the best book ever. It's romance and sci-fi at the same time!" said Violet, dreamily. "Science is the best lesson ever!"

"Science, HA! Who likes science?"

Violet stared at him again.

"My bad."

"I actually have a small question for you," said Violet

"Go on."

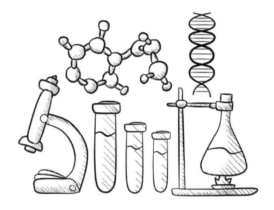

"What's all about the pants?"

"What pants?" Peter hoped Violet would forget about it. He spun around so his back faced Violet. "There's no use turning around! I know you have them. I saw them!"

"You're right. I should tell you," he cleared his throat. "I want to try and prove to everyone that we are all and should be different. I am starting a new school tomorrow at Top High."

"I go there as well!" Violet exclaimed. "I can show you

around!"

"That would be an honour," said Peter as he pretended to
bow.

Violet checked her watch.

"I have to go now as my mum wants me to be home by 9:00.
But here's a quick tip; don't go to school tomorrow wearing
those pants!"

CHAPTER 2
FIRST DAY

"BREAKFAST IS READY, VIVI!" Mrs. Johnson said.

"I'M COMING, MUM!"

She ran down the stairs in a hurry, hoping she had enough time before school to have a calm, nutritious, breakfast. It

was her favourite; toast with peanut butter. She turned to look at her brother but he backed away.

"Move back, you know I'm allergic!"

"Ha, sorry," Violet laughed, her eyes glued to her brother's plate.

"You really like that, don't you?" He shrugged.

"Yeh, I guess so," he said. You could see bits of bread as he talked. Chocolate spread could be seen smudged all over his face. Violet gobbled her food up, grabbed her stuff, and started to run to school. She was so excited to see her new friend.

Meanwhile, on the other side of her street, Peter Simons was running as well to get to school. Unfortunately, it took him exactly 1 hour, 33 minutes and 47 seconds to get there.

Within that period, he travelled to India, met a man called

Rash, who sold rash cream. He also met a woman called Barbara, who sold bras, and then came back to find himself right where he left off.

"Great," He said sarcastically. "Just the luck I needed on my first day." Instead of going and getting lost again, he asked his parents to take him there.

Peter and his parents were greeted by the headteacher, Mr. Scott. Some kids standing behind him, holding up posters that said "Top Highs ratings" while Mr. Scott talked away. Peter wasn't concentrating on most of what he was saying

but the last words got stuck in his head: "Reach High At Top High!" At the end of the speech, Mr. Scott asked him. "Are you excited to start?" Peter replied, "Uhhh....reach high at Top High?" "I think he's ready! Violet, come show Peter around!"

"Sure." She winked at Peter.

CHAPTER 3
THE MEAN TWINS

"Nobody has noticed yet, Violet!" said Peter.

"Notice what?" Peter pulled Violet to the nearest wall and showed her what he was referring to.

"Peter! I told you not to wear your pants yesterday!"

"I had to. I couldn't resist!"

"Just don't show anyone," cried Violet. "Well, we better get on with the tour, we don't want to be late for class."

Violet had shown him nearly every classroom until they got stopped.

"Oh hey, nerd, who's this? Your new, little wizard friend?" One girl said.

"I am not a wizard!" Peter complained.

"Oh yea, I just remembered you're more of a baby wizard with no brain," the other stated. She began to mimic a baby's voice. "Googoo gaagaa!I am a baby and I cry all the time!"

Peter held his tears in. "Good one, Mila."

"Get out of our way!" Violet cried.

"Fine, we will go, but try not to bring your cry baby friend with you next time, nerd." They walked away.

"Who were they?" Peter questioned.

"Lila and Mila. They are the school bullies. Try not to bump into them by the gym as they are always there."

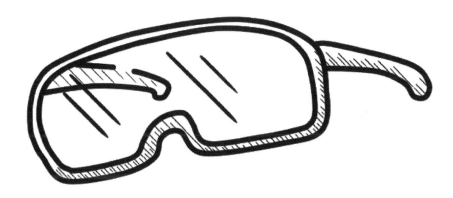

Finally, they reached Violet's favourite place of the tour, the science department!

"This is where I hang out most of the time. It's my favourite place in the entire school!"

"This....is not really my comfort zone," Peter said.

"Don't worry, you're going to love it!" Violet swung open the doors and the first thing she saw was a place filled with mystery and destruction.

"Oops, I forgot to mention, that's my best friend, Jessie."

"Hi Violet," Jessie said. "Who is this?"

"This is Peter. I met him yesterday!"

"Cool! Does he know about thingie?"

 "Do I know about what?"

"My 101 goldfish, of course!" Peter gave a puzzled look. "Let me explain."

"Well, it all started when I was born. We had a beautiful house near the aquarium. Every so often, my family and I would go there and see the fish swim. I liked to focus on them to see poop coming out of their bodies, but my mum

and dad said it was inappropriate. However, one day, while we were at the aquarium, my parents left me looking at the fishes. But as they were gone, I had to cope with more bad news. The aquarium was shutting down!"

I was too sad to notice that the fishes were being taken away one by one. In the end, they were left with only 100 goldfish. Except, the aquarium had other plans with it.

"No one would want them," they cried.

"Let's just chuck them," they cried.

If only they knew I was there!"

"When they had chucked the bag by the dump, it became my chance to leave the place. I thought that I should wear a disguise so no one knew it was me. So, I grabbed some of the aprons from the cafe and started to head out of the aquarium. Of course, I couldn't leave all the goodies

from the sea store behind, right? Well, I grabbed one of everything and headed for the dump. It was Operation Grab-The-Fish next!"

When no one was looking, I snuck over to the dump. In stealth speed, my hand grabbed the bag of fish and stuffed it down my apron. To be honest, I looked very

grownup as I had seemed to have grown two bumps on my body.

"Ewww," said Peter

"I know, right? I still had more steps on my challenge."

Creeping back to my house would be the problem. I

think I had overdressed and I was getting weird stares, so I transformed the apron into a small carrier bag and headed home. Then I got into the house without being noticed. I ran to the back door, but it was locked. I had to find another way in. Then it hit me. My window! And the great thing was that it was half-open.

I snuck into my room; happy to find Jerry, my own other goldfish in his tank.

"I shall pour the other fish into Jerry's tank!" I cried. I had only one more step of my quest!"

"The last step of my mission would be brave indeed!" "What

was it?" Peter questioned.

"Telling my parents, of course!"

"What did they do to you?"

"Oh, nothing really. Just a "GO TO YOUR ROOM!" and a

screen ban for a week." "That was the best adventure story ever!"

"Just remember, if someone doesn't know about my goldfish, tell them the story!"

CHAPTER 5
THE ANNOUNCEMENT

The bell rang as soon as they reached the classroom. Peter stared around him. Some kids were scattered all over the place. Dusty maps of each continent were placed around the room, books were stacked on every desk, and the chairs were a weird shade of red. Also, the fire extinguisher was on its last life. Everything was like a normal classroom, apart from the teacher.

Mrs. Rowe had short, dead straight, blond hair. Her blue eyes glistened as she stared at the clock. She wore a green top with a knot on the front and denim blue jeans. Her

bandana was placed perfectly in her hair, which looked

like a finishing touch on a cake. Mrs. Rowe was one of the prettiest teachers that Peter had ever seen!

"Good morning class. Today, we will be welcoming a new

student. His name is Peter." "More like a "Cry Baby"!" said Mila. The whole class laughed. Peter turned red.

"Inappropriate Mila, detention!"

"But.."

"No buts! Anyway, Peter, take a seat next to Lila."

"Why do I have to sit next to a wizard boy?" Lila said sarcastically "Detention for you as well Lila! You should know better!"

"But mum.."

"Mum?" Peter whispered to Violet.

"Yep. Mrs. Rowe is their mum."

"OK class, let's start the register."

Just after they had finished, an announcement came through from the principal.

"Good morning Top High. Today, I am announcing

that we will be holding our school council tryouts on Friday afternoon at 13:00. Make sure to prepare a good speech.

It can be about something you want to change about the school, something you want to happen, or something you are planning to change everyone's minds about. Get cracking as

you only have 4 days!"

Peter's mind began buzzing with thoughts. 'This could be my chance. Maybe for once everyone would listen and agree with me. Maybe I can become a sensation for kids. Maybe everyone could change their mind about me,' he thought to himself.

"Violet," he whispered. "This could be our chance!"

CHAPTER 6
MEET SEB

"Why are you dragging me to the study room?" Violet

questioned. "If we want them to change, we gotta make
that speech."

"I know that! I mean, why are you dragging me?'

"Oh!" Peter did not know what to say.

"Anyway, do you even know what you are going to write
about?" "Well, er.." Again, he was speechless.

"Let me slow this down. What do you want to change?"

Peter had many ideas written down. He kept dozing off,
thinking about bananas, but in the end, he managed to

finish his long list. It was full of power and bananas.

"Hey! I told you not to put bananas!" Violet didn't even think they were going to be able to write this with only the two of them. After much thinking and consideration, she had a plan.

"Wait a sec, let me go fetch someone."

"Who?" But before he could say any more, she was gone.

"This is my brother, Sebastian."

"Call me Seb for short," he mumbled. Peter could tell that he wouldn't like Seb.

"Huh? Why is he here?" Peter questioned.

"I asked him to help us."

"Well then, what are we waiting for?" Seb cried.

"Seb, you need to be patient! This is not a race."

"Fine, just tell me the ideas. I don't have the time!"

"What? You're going off to watch Peppa Pineapple?" Peter

asked sarcastically. Seb gave Peter a long, harsh stare.

"You're going down!" Seb mouthed.

"Oh, you're going down!" he mouthed back. But Peter didn't know he would regret saying that for the rest of his life.

CHAPTER 7
SEBS PLAN

The next day, Peter felt very sick, or let's just say what he told his parents. However, on Violet and Seb's side, they were having a day off. Their parents thought they needed a rest. Peter just told his parents that he was going to get a pill for his stomach and climbed up the window leading to Seb and Violet's room. This was the second day of writing

the speech.

"How did you get up here?" Seb said, rolling his eyes.

"Oh, don't you question me!"

"Boys, stop arguing! You guys are so immature!" Violet

shook her head. "Anyway, we should
be getting on with this. You know this
is your only opportunity, Peter."
"Fine," he said. "Let's get started!"
"We will begin with the intro." Then,
they started writing. Seb wouldn't
dare to watch them, so he had a
plan. He thought to himself, 'If I
make some sort of disgusting and

powerful substance, I could destroy those underpants and
all his rest for good! Peter would also have nothing to prove

his answers!' He grinned. He slid out of their room and went to find some of his disliked paint.

"I knew you would come in handy one day!" he whispered. He squirted the paint into a bucket and was about to pour the paint into some gooey slime when he noticed that Peter was looking at what he was doing. Before he could have a clear view, Seb hid behind their bedroom door.

"OK, halfway done! But where is Seb?"

"I don't know and I don't care!"

"Well, you don't need to care because I am right here!" Seb said, coming out from behind the door. "Why were you down there?" Peter questioned.

"I thought you said you didn't care."

"Well, I would care if you two don't stop arguing! Read what we have done so far and tell us if it would be good for the school."

"No no no, you can't send it like this!"

"Why not?" "Because people may think it's weird and inappropriate that you have mentioned underpants."

"But it's just the truth!" Peter told him.

"I admit though, it is a good idea."

"Well, thanks? I guess…" Seb didn't let Peter finish his statement.

"But here are my tips. Don't talk about underpants, don't wear underpants on the outside, and don't tell ANYONE about how you wear your underpants until the day!"

"But…"

"GO!" Seb screamed, and Peter climbed out.

"You were really harsh," Violet said. "Thanks a lot." For the first time, Seb felt bad.

CHAPTER 8
THE ARGUMENT

The next day, it began raining HEAVILY! The sky was misty

and grey as water clogged the sewage pipes. Streets were being flooded and raincoats and wellies were the town's armour. The rain swept down, ready to pounce sadness on the people. The sun was as miserable as Violet, and she was very miserable as well!

Peter did not talk or walk near her for the whole day. He didn't even stare at her! At the end of the day, Violet decided it was best to ask if they were going to meet up to do more of the speech. She slowly approached him and before she could say anything, he rolled his eyes and said,

"What do you want?"

"I was just wondering if we were going to carry on the speech today."

"But, will it be at your house?"

"I mean, we can always change the location. Didn't you like it there the last time? Did you find it stinky?"

"The stinky one is your brother," he muttered.

"What did you say?"

"The only problem is your brother!"

"He saw me peeking through his door,

but I felt that he was hiding something from us. We need to figure out what he is trying to do!"

"That can't be true! My brother would never do such a thing."

"The thing is, he is doing it already. And we NEED to find out!"

"How do you know?"

"Because I saw him and…"

"That's your only proof? Seb pushed his way in front of Violet and turned to face her. "Would you actually believe that LIAR against you brother!

"Ahhh, the sweet sound of the voice of Seb Johnson. How lovely of you to interrupt our conversation!" Peter sang. Seb was getting really annoyed and Violet could tell.

"Stop it, Peter!" Violet cried.

"I am telling you for the last time that he's lying!" Peter confessed

"Shut up idiot!"

"Violet, why does your stupid brother have to ruin my life just as it starts to get exciting? Bullies just always come for me!"

"What do you mean?" Violet questioned.

"At my old school, I was normal until I got bullied. I thought all their cool shorts were underpants, so one day I turned up to school wearing them. Then, I got bullied for being different, but I was starting to like that."

"That is sad but why did you call my brother stupid!"

"It's true!" Peter cried

"This is just getting boring!" Violet said. But Peter wasn't bored yet!

Peter and Seb were arguing way too much for Violet to take, so she shouted,

"Will you guys ever stop arguing? I don't want to believe anyone, OK!"

"I thought you just said that your brother would never do such a thing! You're on his side and that's evident!" Upset by the whole scenario, Peter walked off.

"He is really sensitive, isn't he?" Violet asked her brother.

"Who cares!" They both went home. But little did they know that at that moment, Peter was planning revenge.

CHAPTER 9
OPERATION SPY

"So, what's in this for me, Peter?" Peter was standing inside Jessie's room (or as she called it, lab). He had managed to convince Jessie to spy on Violet and Seb.

"I will give you the latest phone. How's that?" It took Jessie no time at all to answer.

"It's a deal! When do I start?"

"Well, the other day, you told me your parents were going on holiday on Tuesday night and it's Tuesday afternoon! You can start today."

"But how?"

"I thought you were a spy? If you were, you would have known that, right?" Jessie didn't want to embarrass herself.

"Oh yes, silly me. I have a plan!"

"I should stay at her house while my parents are gone. It's only for two days, anyway. But the only problem is that I am meant to be staying with my grandma. What should I do?"

"How about a robot!" Peter exclaimed. "Have you ever made one?"

"Yes."

"Could you make one now?"

"It may take me a couple of hours but I will do it for that phone."

"But do you actually know why you are making it?" It took Jessie a couple of seconds to realise Peter's plan.

"So you're saying my grandma will have a robot version of me?"

"I mean yeah, they're old, anyway. It should do the trick. You ready?" Jessie's mind began buzzing with thoughts. Keep your eyes on the prize, Jessie. It's only for two days and this will be finished in no time! "Yes!" she replied. Then, they got started. Peter went into another room

whilst Jessie worked in her room.

"This is what I have done so far, Peter." It had been about an hour since Peter had arrived; spending most of his time watching TV. He stared at the figure she was holding. It shined as she moved it around. Its arms and legs were not yet complete but Peter was absolutely gobsmacked.

"Uhh, are you OK?"

"Yeh, that is so cool! Can I touch it?" With that, he leaned forward to touch it. Jessie rapidly pulled it away from him.

"You can't touch it! It's too delicate." Peter groaned. The

thought of the phone rushed into Jessie's head. "But you can help me test it out?" Peter cheered.

"Now, just let me finish it off and I will be right back!"

Five minutes later, Jessie appeared with the robot.

"Told ya I would be right back!" she giggled. "Let's test it out!"

"OK," Peter said. "How do we start?"

"First, what we are going to do is drop it out of the window!"

"WHAT!" Peter was horrified, "WHY! WHY WOULD YOU DO THAT TO SOMETHING SO GOOD?"

"Ha, got you there!" Peter shook his head with anger. "What we really have to do is just watch it walk around the room to

see if I have programmed it right!" And when she clicked the button, the magic began...

"OMG, IT CAN WALK!" Peter was joyfully frightened. "Yay, I programmed it right for the first time today!" "What do you mean by "the first time?"

"Oh, just had some explosions and..."

"EXPLOSIONS?" Peter was furious.

"How was I even too busy to hear them."

"They were silent... but violent!" she giggled. "Get it?"

"Just don't talk about it again, I get worried about myself even though it didn't hit me!" "Well, we're done with the robot!" Jessie said excitedly. "And you know what that means…" "Yes, it's time for you to pack. You're leaving any minute. OPERATION: Get cracking!"

CHAPTER 10
ROBOT DROP OFF

Ding Dong!

"Why are you here, Jessie?" Mrs. Johnson questioned.

"My mum and dad are going on holiday and I have nowhere to stay. Can I stay at yours?" "Sure, come inside!" Jessie picked up her stuff and went in.

"I will set up a bed for you so you can have some time to settle in."

"I have to quickly go get my pillow as I left it at home. Can I please go get it?"

"OK, but be quick!"

"I will!" Then, she ran out of the house.

"Peter, are you reading? Peter, are you reading?" she whispered to her headset.

"Yes, reading!" Peter called back. "Just to say, why are you so loud?"

"Because we are standing in front of each other!" Peter stared ahead and removed his headset.

"OK, you are allowed to stay, right?" Peter took a deep breath. He knew that if she had said no, the plan would be ruined. He thought to himself, 'I think she will let her in. They are best friends.'

"Yep. Just told her I was going to get my pillow. Shall we drop off you-know-what?" Peter swallowed hard.

"Oh, I'm ready!"

"OK, we're here!"

"Wow, your grandma's house is MASSIVE!"

I know, right?" Peter took a moment to take in the fantastic view of the house. On the sides of the door were two magnificent fountains with freshwater pouring out. The wooden-glazed front door had a brand-new looking doorknob. The paths had shiny cobblestone; so shiny that

one could even see their reflection! Behind the house was could see a crystal-clear swimming pool with delicate lounge chairs. Peter couldn't believe this was his friend's grandma's house!

"Listen up, we will have to pretend we are my mum and dad!

"Won't she notice?"

"No, she's slightly blind. Go on then, ring the doorbell!"

"Let's go!"

 "Hello, sweet child!" Jessie's grandma said croakily. She hugged the robot. "Grown muscles, haven't you?" Jessie coughed, trying to sound like her mum.

"Yes, she has, mum. Oh no, look at the time! We better get going because we don't want to miss the flight, don't we honey?" Jessie nudged Peter.

"Uhhh...yes, goodbye granny."

"It's Joanne!" Jessie whispered to Peter.

"Oh yes! Sorry, Joanne," Peter said. Jessie wanted to get this done. "Bye!" They walked away.

"What did you do that for?" Jessie cried.

"You didn't tell me her name!"

"Anyway, when we left, I turned on the switch at Violet's house, so I could control her. Talking about Violet's house, I need to get going. She will probably be wondering where I am." Without thinking, she put in her earpiece and started to head off.

"Peter, make sure we chat on here when we need to. See you soon!" Peter said to himself.

"I better get going too. I wouldn't want my mum to start worrying about me!"

"Why did you take so long? And where is your pillow?"

"Oh, my mum and dad took all the pillows on holiday and I ended up spending ages looking for nothing!" "Oh OK. I have set up your bed for you. Go get ready for bed, it's quite late."

"I do need the loo, can I go?"

"Yes, this time, be quick!" Jessie ran into the bathroom. She

quickly coded the robot to do what she would do for bed. She flushed the chain, turned the tap on and off, and ran upstairs. Violet's mum already told Violet that Jessie was here. They both agreed to go to bed. She thought it was time to get some sleep. 'I have a busy day ahead of me!'

CHAPTER 11
SUSPICION

"Morning Violet!"

"Morning Jessie!" Violet seemed to be in a really good mood today.

"Morning Jessica," Seb said, trying to annoy her purposely.

"You know my name is Jessie, it even says so on my birth certificate!" She rolled her eyes. "Can you please leave us alone, Seb?"

"Why would I? This is also my room!"

That is true," Jessie said. "But Seb, I need some help on my art project, can you help me?" "Sure. Not like I have anything else to do!"

"OK. First, I need to find some paint!"

"OK."

"How about this one?" Seb gulped. It was the one he was

trying to use for Peter's underpants.

"We have plenty of other better paints! Why choose that one when there are so many better ones!" Jessie could tell he was up to something, so she carried on.

"But that is my favourite!"

"Sorry, I am already using it for another project." Which was somewhat true.

"Oh OK, I will just have to find that paint somewhere else."

Seb remembered that he had put in
slime so there is no other paint of that
kind.

"It's not the paint that I bought. Uhh, I
just mixed some random colours." Jessie
had an idea. She carefully took hold of
the paint and put it in her pocket without
his knowledge.

"Oh, well, I better get going. Bye." And Seb didn't suspect a
thing!

"Peter, Peter, are you reading?"

"Yes, I am. Any information?

"Yes! He is hiding something. But he didn't know that I
actually took it!" "Well done, what does it look like?"

"Well, it's a really pretty shade of emerald, it has chunky bits
of light green and
some sort of sizzling
powder."

"What did you say?" Peter questioned.

"Let's just meet outside." they proceeded to meet each other!

"OK, take a look at this!"

"Wow, this is cool... but disgusting!"

"I know! I could suspect something when I mentioned it. He didn't really know what to say when I brought it up."

"Well, good job for your first task complete!"

"We are not done with this!" Jessie stated.

"How?"

"We need to figure out what this means, and I have just the plan!"

"This is a website I use all the time because without Violet, I have no idea about a thing of science!" "Woah, I thought you loved science?"

"No, I love computer science!"

"Oh, silly me!"

"Anyway, back to the topic. All you have to do is take a photo of anything and it will tell you what it means." FLASH! Information came pouring into the phone like they were rushing for the last ice-cream!

"Hmmm, all the information simply means a way to destroy fabric or cotton. What do you have that's fabric or cotton?" Peter gulped.

"Oh no!"

CHAPTER 12
THE TEA HAS BEEN SPILLED

At school the next day, Jessie thought it was the right time to speak up. "Violet, we need to talk," Jessie said to her.

"About what?"

"About this!" And she lifted up a pot of paint, the pot from Seb!

"That thing could destroy my top, get it away from me!"

"Exactly!"

"Why are you blaming me like this is my fault?"

"It's not yours, but your brother!"

"What has my brother done?" Jessie pointed to the bottom of the jar. "Read this! You'll see!"

"On the day of school council, pour this on Peter's undies!?"

"You see!"

"What? Peter was telling the truth all along?"

"Yes, and this is the evidence."

"But why?"

"Read the last bit."

"Operation: LET ME WIN!" Violet was shocked.

"Peter and my brother are running for school council?"

"Yep!"

"And he was trying to stop Peter?"

"Yep."

"I can't believe he would do that! But why didn't he tell me?"

"He's your brother. What do you expect?"

"I expected better of him. I thought he would tell me

everything." Violet started to cry.

"Don't cry," Jessie told her, "He has done stuff without telling you before. It's just what people do." "But the thing is, he could have told me that he was trying to write his own!" Jessie smiled.

"Why don't you calmly talk to him?"

"Good idea!"

After school, Violet approached Seb.

"Hi Seb, I have something to tell you."

"What? I'm trying to look for something." He carried on searching and began panicking.

"I know what you're looking for!" Violet told him,

holding up the paint.

"How?" Seb scrunched his face up in confusion.

"Jessie took it. She knew something wasn't right, so she took it, investigated it, and told me. The bottom told me something I thought you would have told me."

"What?"

"That you were going for school council as well, silly! That's why you two were always arguing. You could have told me. Plus, I could have helped you like I was trying to help Peter." Seb gave her a stare and slightly smiled.

"You would have helped me?"

"Yes! I would have been happy to. It's not like I was trying out myself!" They both laughed.

"Well, to be honest, I don't think I have enough time to even write a speech, I better just not try out." His smile faded. "What if you helped Peter? It would make up for your rudeness before to him."

"You know what, Violet? I will!"

CHAPTER 13
FORGIVENESS

Peter was sitting in misery wondering if the plan would work.

He thought if Jessie would be able to convince Violet. 'Will Seb tell the truth? Will Violet believe us?' Peter had no idea who was going to help him, rather than hurt him. He had no idea that his enemy could become his friend. He had no idea that the truth was a shock. He had no idea that his life was about to change! (OK, maybe I overexaggerated about his life changing, but it was fun to say)

"Hey, errr, Pete…"

"I prefer to be called Peter, Seb. What are you doing here, anyway? You too, Violet." Violet explained the whole story to Peter.

"....And then I found out that he was running for school council!"

"Wow!" He did not expect that!

"And then................" By the end of the story, Peter looked as if he was about to pass out.

"And that's when he realised that there was no point running for it as he has no speech with no proof, so we came up with an idea!"

"Go on, Seb, tell him!" Violet ushered him forward.

"Well.."

"Go on then!" Peter leaned further in his chair.

"I decided that to pay off for the things I did to you, and as I don't have to write my own, that I would help you write your speech."

"You would do that for me?" Peter asked.

Violet started to laugh.

"That's exactly what he asked when I said I would have helped him! Now, we better get started. We don't want to waste any time, do we? The school council tryouts are tomorrow! Let's get going!"

About 20 minutes later, Jessie came in.

"So, how's it going?" Jessie announced, walking up to the trio.

"Brilliant! We are so nearly done!" Peter said, with glee.

"'That's great to hear! When will you give me you know what?" Peter gave a 'this is not the right time' stare at Jessie.

"What- you-know-what?" Violet questioned. Peter had no

hope now. He knew Jessie would say EVERYTHING. It's just her personality. And to make matters a fact, she did!

"The phone Peter promised to get me after I had spied on you two!" Peter knew now everything would go wrong!

"You spied on us?" Seb and Violet said in unity.

"It was only to see if anything was up with Seb. Plus, it's all over now!"

"Or is it?"

"What do you mean, Jessie?"

"You know, the robot at granny's?"

"What is going on, Peter?"

"I will explain later, Violet. Jessie, remember to pick up the robot on your way back. I will get the phone ready tomorrow." He really didn't. "When will we finish this though, Peter?"

"Don't worry, I will finish it later by myself. Anyway, what will you do with that icky paint, Seb?" "Oh, don't worry, I have a plan!"

CHAPTER 14
PREPARED FOR TAKE OFF

Peter woke up to the sound of his ultra-noisy-ment-for-school-council-days alarm and rushed out of bed. He put on his smartest school clothes (which to be honest, was

just like the non-fancy ones) and went to fetch his fanciest pants. He came back into his room with a pair of black and

white striped undies with a silky trim. He looked very smart, compared to how he usually appeared.

Next, Peter ran to the bathroom. He thought to himself, 'I can't let smelly breath pull me down from winning,' so he brushed his teeth five times! He slipped his shoes on, tightened up his tie, grabbed the least smelly fruit he had, and ran out of the door.

Whilst Peter was making sure he was early, the two siblings and Jessie were working their butts off. Violet and Seb were making gallons of the icky stuff, whilst Jessie was fetching every pair of underpants from her house, making sure she didn't forget one. Once they were done, the three of them

met up at school to begin their plan. And at the same time, Peter coincidentally arrived too! However, Peter knew what was happening.

"Chop chop, everybody!" Seb announced. Peter appeared in front of him.

"You're early!" Jessie stated.

"I know, I didn't want to be late."

"Then, you can be useful and help us take this to the roof of the gym," Seb told him. "Why are you doing that?"

"Because Mila is running for school council and we can't let that happen! Right, Seb?"Violet spoke up. "Yes."

"But why the roof?"

"So, we will be near the big pipes to put the goo and pants in.

Come on, what are you waiting for?"

They all ran up to the top in a hurry. They had all agreed that Jessie would stay on the roof, so she could be the one to pour the stuff on top of Mila!

"Yay, I like my job! I get to miss lessons!"

"Sorry, there are no lessons, only Form Room. It's the first thing today!" Jessie's smile faded, then appeared again. "But I still get to pour goo on Mila, and that's a good thing!"

"Agreed. Now, get on the roof! Remember to talk on your headset!" Peter exclaimed.

"I think we should all hide before the kids start piling through." But it had already happened!

The doors started to open. The hurricane had returned to the school. Kids were everywhere. Books clattered as Mila and Lila through kids to the floor. They kept on saying,

"You better vote for us or you'll get bullied for the whole of this year!" The three friends pushed their way to

the Science Department, where no one was.

"OK, we know the plan, right?"

"Yep, sure do, Seb!"

"We have all the supplies on the roof?"

"Yep!"

"Well, there is only one thing." Seb turned to Peter, "Good luck!"

CHAPTER 15
READY, SET, SPEECH!

All the kids were already called into the hall. It was time for the school council tryouts! With their heads held high, most of the youngsters who were trying out were rehearsing their lines so it would be perfect. But some weren't. Some were panicking. Some were trying hard to memorise them, but the

words wouldn't get in their heads. Peter was one of such. His hands were shaking in fear, but he knew he had his friends. He was worried he was too new, but he could be better than others. He began to take his seat when the first person started. "...And that is my speech!" Everyone clapped.

"That was good, wasn't it, Violet?"

"Yes, sure was."

"I hope mine is better!"

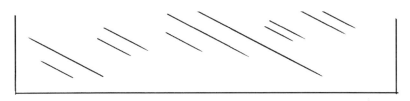

"Girls, boys, stop whispering! It is other people's time to shine! Don't ruin it for them," Mrs. Rowe told the school.

The first five people had finished and Peter was already wondering when it would be his turn. His ears were listening out for one word, which was when their project would begin. One more person went by. Peter told Seb,

"Is Mila ever going to go?" And sure enough, the next thing they heard was,

"Next up, Mila!"

"Operation slime in.."

"Hey, I'm Mila,"

"3..."

"And if you don't vote for me," "2..."

 "I will bully you for a year."

"1..."

"Because-"

"GO!" Peter whispered into the headset. Jessie replied saying, "I'm on it!" She poured half of the slime through the pipes "Any

minute now, the slime would pour right on top of her!"

I will help everyone..." And at that exact moment, the slime fell

all over her. The whole hall was in hysterics, apart from Lila.

"ARGHHHHHHH" Mila screamed.

"OMG, WHAT HAPPENED MILA?" Lila ran over to see if she was OK.

"Jessie, pour the next lot down!" Peter told the headset again. "Got it!" Jessie poured the last half of the bucket. Lila was positive to find where it was coming from. She looked around the room and when she stared at the ceiling, the last lot of slime toppled all over her, especially on her face!

"WHOEVER DID THIS WILL PAY!" Lila cried as she ran out of the hall with Mila.

"We have had a bit of a problem, so we will move on to our last person, Peter!"

"Hi." Peter swallowed. He was panicking but at the same time, trying to stay calm.

"Today, I will be talking about why you should choose me. Usually, people say if you pick me, there will be no more homework or no more school, but that's not how I work. I leave it up to you to vote about anything you want, then I make the final decision. I want to be different. I want you to be different. And you didn't know that I am different every day by doing this!" Peter gulped and lifted up his cloak. Everyone was shocked. Violet gave the signal and Jessie dropped the underpants down. Peter picked one up and showed it to the rest of the school.

"As you can see, that is my touch of uniqueness. I wear what I feel proud to wear on the front and I want you to not be a dull person. If you vote for me, you will always be yourself with me, no matter what. Thank you for listening and I hope you vote for me! And always remember, the difference is that I am different!"

The hall gave a massive roar of applause. Peter did not expect to get so much appreciation of his speech. The kids were cheering and even the adults were clapping.

"Well, I guess we'll just have to ask you guys one thing. Whose votes are for Peter?" Everyone's hands went up. "That's great news. Peter, you are Top Highs new school council!" Mr. Scott announced. The school gave another applause. Violet and Seb ran to him and gave him a massive hug.

"Thanks for helping me win, guys!"

"No problem!" They both said. Peter looked around the hall to see Jessie even dancing and cheering on the roof.

"I guess hard work always pays off!" he took a deep breath and smiled.

CHAPTER 16

THE LAST CHAPTER

The bell rang! It was the end of the day. The hall began to get empty real quick. Some kids were meeting up with their parents, hugging them, and flooding off. Others were lining

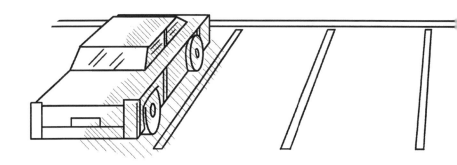

up to get on the squashed school bus. The teachers pulled up in their cars to go off. They all mainly have kids, so there was no time to be wasted! The car park was pretty much empty at

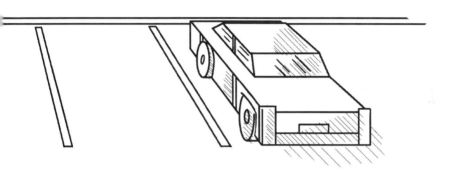

this point. In the distance, Peter could see someone coming up to him. It looked like Mrs. Rowe. He wanted to hide but didn't get there in time.

"Well done, Peter! You were very good out there!"

"Uhhhh, thanks?"

"Are you excited to be our new school council?"

"Yes. I mean, I did really want to be it but didn't expect myself to win!" "Are you proud of yourself?" Mrs. Rowe asked.

"Well, yes, I mean..."

"That's great Peter! Well, I need to be on my way with Mila and Lila. Bye!" She walked away with Mila and Lila trailing behind,

making silly faces at Peter. They were annoyed he won but they didn't know that he was the one who did the goo!

Eventually, the school was empty. There were no cars in sight. Jessie was looking a bit worried.

"Where's my mum and dad? They were meant to come from the airport to pick us up by now!" "I don't know," Violet replied, looking around.

"They better be here soon. I am starving!" Seb mumbled. Everyone laughed.

"You know what guys, we could all just walk home, right?" Peter asked.

"Only if they don't turn up," said Violet.

"Which they probably won't!" Everyone burst into giggles again! Violet went back to trying to find Jessie's parents. Then her eyes spotted a car.

"Is that it?" Violet asked.

"You have known me long enough, Violet. Of course, it is!"

Jessie's mum and dad parked and jumped out of the car.

"Sorry we're late hun, we just went home to put everything back."

"That's OK, not like I cared," Jessie told them.

"I did!" Seb announced, trying to be funny. But no one took any notice of him.

"Darling, why are there slimy footprints coming out of the hall?" Everyone looked at Peter. He was the best at making up stories.

"Well you see, to celebrate school council, the teachers

decided to get slimed! It was so funny, wasn't it guys?" They all repeated,

"Yes, it was hilarious!"

"Oh, goodie good! Well, everyone get in the car, we don't want your parents to be worried

They all hopped in the car and sat down.

"So, how was school sweetie?"

"It was good, mum. My new friend, Peter, won the school council!"

"Well done!" Jessie's dad said.

"Thanks." Peter was smiling.

"Did you do anything else?"

"Yes, I got to slime the teachers!" Everyone laughed.

"You know, today was the best day ever, especially how I got to spend it with you guys!"

"Yes, same!" Seb said. The car came to a halt as they landed at Violet's house. Jessie's mum chimed in, "I guess this is your stop. Jessie, say bye to your friends."

"Bye guys."

"Bye Jessie!" And they left the car. Jessie's parents turned to

face her. Jessie could tell something was wrong.

"So honey, when we got home to put everything away and got in new clothes, and we noticed that our underpants draws were empty. Have you seen our pants anywhere?" Her dad asked.

"Uhoh!"